HA ᴀᵀᴱ iET'S
1999
RE

BY THE SAME AUTHOR

Babe: The Gallant Pig

Harry's Mad

Martin's Mice

Ace: The Very Important Pig

The Toby Man

Paddy's Pot of Gold

Pretty Polly

The Invisible Dog

Three Terrible Trins

DICK KING-SMITH
HARRIET'S HARE

ILLUSTRATED BY ROGER ROTH

CROWN PUBLISHERS, INC., NEW YORK

Published by Crown Publishers, Inc., a Random House company,
201 East 50th Street, New York, New York 10022

CROWN is a trademark of Crown Publishers, Inc.

Manufactured in the United States of America

Library of Congress Cataloging-in-Publication Data
King-Smith, Dick.
Harriet's hare / by Dick King-Smith ; illustrated by Roger Roth.
p. cm.
Summary: A young girl's life with her father on their farm in
England is changed when she befriends a talking hare that is really
a shape-changing alien.
[1. Extraterrestrial beings—Fiction. 2. Hares—Fiction. 3. Farm life—
England—Fiction. 4. England—Fiction.] I. Roth, Roger, ill. II. Title.
PZ2.K5893Hap 1995
[Fic]—dc20 94-20378
ISBN 0-517-59830-2 (trade)
0-517-59831-0 (lib. bdg.)

10 9 8 7 6 5 4 3 2

HARRIET'S HARE

CHAPTER ONE

Harriet sat up, suddenly wide awake.

What was that noise?

It was a rushing, tearing, swishing noise, just like the sound fireworks make, yet much, much louder. But this was the start of a midsummer day and—Harriet looked at her watch—early, too, not even five o'clock.

She leaped out of bed and ran to the window.

The farmhouse and its buildings were tucked into the side of a gentle hill, and in the flat little valley below were two large fields, the nearer green, the farther gold.

In the first, her father's cows would normally have been waiting around the gateway for him to come and fetch them in for morning milking. But now the whole herd was galloping and buck-jumping around the pasture as though something had scared the wits out of them.

The second field was of wheat, almost ready for harvesting, that looked from the house like a square golden blanket glowing in the morning sunlight. But there seemed to be a hole in the blanket. In one corner of the field, Harriet could see, there was a perfect circle of flattened wheat.

It took Harriet fifteen minutes to dress and slip out of the house and run down the dewy hillside. By now the cows had quieted, and she ran past them to the field beyond, then climbed over its gate and pushed through the standing wheat to step into that perfect circle.

What had made it? What had made the noise that had woken her and terrified the cows? What had happened in the field called Ten Acre on Longhanger Farm at the start of this July day?

Harriet walked into the middle of the circle. It was big, perhaps sixty feet across, and all the wheat in it was squashed down flat to the ground as though an enormously heavy weight had stood there.

As she stood there now in the stillness, with no sound but distant birdsong, a hare suddenly came out into the circle and stopped and sat up. It turned its head a little sideways, the better to see her.

Harriet stood perfectly still. Aren't you handsome, she thought, with your tawny coat and your black-tipped ears and your long hind legs. Don't run away. I won't hurt you.

3

For a moment the hare stayed where it was, watching her. Then, to her great surprise, it lolloped right up to her.

Surprise is one thing, but total amazement is quite another, and that was what Harriet felt next when all of a sudden the hare said, loudly and clearly, "Good morning."

Harriet pinched herself—hard. Wake up, she thought. This whole thing is a dream. Hares don't talk. And aloud she said, "Hares don't talk."

"I'm sure they don't as a general rule," said the hare, "but I'm a rather unusual hare."

"You certainly are," said Harriet. "Do you have anything to do with this circle?"

For a moment the hare did not answer but instead began grooming its face.

Then it said, "What's your name?"

"Harriet."

"Can you keep a secret, Harriet?"

"Yes."

"I," said the hare, "am a visitor from outer space."

"You mean . . . this circle was made by your spaceship?"

"Yes."

"So you come from another planet?"

"Yes. I come from Pars."

"Pars?" said Harriet. "Is that near Mars?"

"Oh, no," said the hare. "Much, much farther away."

"But," said Harriet, "I thought that aliens were, well, little and green and had four arms and eyes on stalks."

"Not far off," said the hare. "But you see, Harriet, we Partians have the ability to change. Imagine how strange your modern world here would seem to cave dwellers. What would they make of microsurgery and satellite television and supersonic flight? You have to understand that on Pars we are as far ahead of you people on Earth as you now are of the cave dwellers. One of the things we can do, for example, is to speak all earthly languages. But, perhaps to you the most astonishing, we have perfected the ability to change our shape. When my colleagues left me here in this wheatfield, I could, for instance, have decided to become a tiger—though that might have caused a bit of a stir in deepest Wiltshire—or a dog or a sheep or anything else you like. But I chose to change myself into a hare."

"Why?" asked Harriet.

"Because in this world the hare has always been thought to be a beast of magic. People said that hares were witches and could melt away and reappear to dance and play in the light of the moon. Incidentally, some people still say that if you look at the full moon, it is not a man's face that you see there, but rather the shape of a hare. And others believed that hares could change their sex at will."

"Oh," said Harriet. "Which are you at the moment?"

"I," said the hare, "am a buck and fully intend to remain so for the length of my stay on Earth."

Harriet suddenly felt terribly disappointed. Here she was, in her father's wheatfield, deep in conversation with a magic hare, but perhaps he would only be around for a very short time.

"How long are you staying?" she asked.

"It depends," said the hare, "on how much I like it here. This is actually my first vacation on Earth."

"You've come here on vacation?" asked Harriet.

"Oh, yes," said the hare. "Everyone on Pars takes a vacation abroad every so often. Interplanetary travel is so quick and easy nowadays, you know—to anywhere in the solar system that you like. I've been to a number of heavenly bodies but never to Earth. I just wanted to go somewhere quite different this year, somewhere rather primitive, where the technology was not very advanced and one could relax among the simple, ignorant natives. So I came here. But that's enough about me, Harriet. Tell me a bit about yourself. All I know is your name."

"Well," said Harriet, "I'm almost eight, and I go to the village school, and my dad's a farmer, and we've got cows and some sheep and some chickens, and Dad works the farm all by himself except sometimes he gets a relief milker in so that we can take a vacation."

"But your mother helps with the animals, I expect?" said the hare.

"My mother's dead," said Harriet. "She died when I was quite little. I don't really remember her. But I help Dad. I look after the hens, and I feed the calves, and this year I bottle-fed three lambs. They'd lost their mother, too."

"You like animals," said the hare.

"Oh, yes. Especially my pony. She's a strawberry roan, twelve and a half hands high. She's called Breeze. By the way, I don't know your name."

"Nor do I," said the hare, "if you see what I mean. On Pars, I had a perfectly good name, but I really haven't given a thought about what to be called now that I am a specimen of *Lepus europaeus occidentalis*."

"What?"

"That's the Latin name for a hare."

"You speak Latin, too?"

"I told you. Partians are omnilingual."

"Oh," said Harriet. "Well, what should I call you?"

"Whatever you like," said the hare. "You choose."

Harriet thought.

A visitor from outer space that speaks all languages, that can transform itself into any shape, a creature of witchcraft, a magician. He's a wizard, that's what he is.

"Wiz," she said.

The hare, who had remained sitting in the middle of the circle throughout the entire conversation, stood up on his long hind legs. His ears raised, his large brown eyes inquiring, he looked the very picture of astonishment.

"Wiz?" he said.

"Yes. That's what I shall call you."

"Oh, very well," sighed Harriet's hare. "Wiz it is."

CHAPTER TWO

Suddenly a dog barked. Harriet turned to see her father coming down the hill toward the cow pasture, the old sheepdog Bran running ahead of him.

Bran's barking said quite clearly, today as every day, "Come along, you silly cows, whatever you're doing—it's time for milking."

And as soon as the farmer opened the gate, Bluebell, the head cow whose right it was to be first through any gateway, began the climb up the path through the paddock, the rest of the herd following behind her.

"That's my dad," said Harriet, but she found she was talking to herself, for the hare had vanished.

She climbed back over the field gate and ran toward her father.

"Hattie!" he called in astonishment. "What in the world are you doing out so early?"

Harriet thought quickly.

"Can you keep a secret?" Wiz had said. She must say nothing about him.

"There's a circle, Dad!" she cried. "In our wheat. I saw it from my bedroom window."

Leaving Bran to take the cows on up the hill, the farmer walked with Harriet to the field.

"I've heard about these, Hattie," he said, "but I've never seen one, except in photos."

"What made it, Dad, d'you think?"

"There are lots of theories. Some say badgers, rolling in the wheat, but it would have taken a hundred giant badgers to make this. Most likely it's caused by a kind of whirling vortex of wind, like a tornado. Though of course there are always the nuts who say that the circles are made by spaceships!"

"That's ridiculous!" said Harriet.

"It is!" said her father.

Somewhere in the standing wheat there was a rustling noise.

"Rabbit in there," said Harriet's father.

"Or a hare perhaps?" said Harriet.

"Could be. They'd better be out of it before I put the combine in."

He takes his gun with him when he rides the combine, Harriet thought. I must warn Wiz.

"When will this field be ready, d'you think?" she asked.

Her father pulled off an ear of wheat, rubbing it between his hands to free the kernels and then chewing them to test their ripeness.

"Not long now," he said.

From the top of the hill Bran barked. Again there was no mistaking his meaning. "The cows are in the yard, I've done my part, what d'you expect me to do now—milk 'em?"

"Come on, Hattie," said Harriet's father. "I've got work to do."

"So do I," said Harriet. "I'm going to load the washing machine before I start making breakfast. And the downstairs needs dusting."

"I'd forgotten," said her father. "It's the start of your school summer vacation, isn't it?"

"Yes," said Harriet. "A woman's work is never done."

A woman! thought her father as he let the first cows into the milking parlor. Poor girl, she's had to grow up fast without a mother. Though I think she's mostly forgotten her now. Which I never shall. But it can't be much fun for Hattie, stuck here alone with me. What she needs is a bit of magic in her life. Children believe in magic. She probably thinks that circle was made by extraterrestrials. Ridiculous.

Later that morning, when the wash was in the dryer and Harriet had flicked a duster about (a woman from the village came twice a week to do the cleaning), she went back down to the circle in the wheatfield.

She half expected to see Wiz waiting for her,

but the circle was empty. Where had he gone? When would she see him again? Would she see him again? Like her, he was on vacation, but the fact that she was staying here on Longhanger Farm didn't mean that he was, too. He could go wherever he liked.

She trudged back across the cow pasture. Wiz might be miles away by now, loping across the hillside, simply enjoying being a hare, with no thought of her at all.

Just then she saw, not fifteen feet away, a brown shape squatting motionless in a clump of grass, long ears flats to its head.

"Wiz!" she cried, and at the sound of her voice the hare leaped up and sped away.

"Come back!" called Harriet, but to no avail, and she felt the prick of tears as the animal disappeared through the nearest hedge.

Wiz didn't want to have anything more to do with her. Never again would she speak with the magical visitor from Pars. Or maybe, thought Harriet, I'm going crazy and I just imagined it all.

"Wrong hare," said a voice behind her.

"Oh, Wiz!" cried Harriet. "Am I glad to see

you! I was beginning to wonder. . . ." She stopped.

"If you'd dreamed the whole thing?" said the hare.

"Yes . . . no . . . I didn't know what to think."

"Did you tell your father about me?"

"No. I promised not to. But Wiz, you must be careful, because soon he'll be harvesting the wheat, and that means he goes around and around the field on a big machine called a combine, and he shoots any rabbit that runs out, especially at the end when there's only a little square of wheat left in the middle. People eat rabbits, you see."

"But I'm not a rabbit."

"Hares, too," said Harriet.

"People eat hares?" said Wiz.

"I'm afraid so. Jugged hare is very good."

"Jugged?"

"Yes. Cut up in pieces and stewed with wine and herbs. Sorry, but they do."

"How primitive!" said Wiz. "So bad for you, all this meat eating. How fortunate that I chose to become a hare and not a tiger. Your grass is really excellent."

"Are you all vegetarians on Pars?" asked Harriet.

"Absolutely. No one kills anything for food."

"But what about wars? People here on Earth are always killing one another."

"So pointless," said Wiz. "You really are still like savages. We Partians like to live as long as possible. Admittedly we haven't yet cracked the riddle of everlasting life, but we like to hope for a couple hundred years or so apiece before we're bottled."

"Bottled?"

"We don't bury bodies or burn them like you barbarians," said the hare. "We preserve our dead in a special solution. Standing upright in bottles."

"They must be very big bottles," said Harriet.

"No. We're very small. All you need is a couple of shelves and you can keep all your ancestors. You never really lose anyone."

How horrible, thought Harriet. She suddenly felt angry.

"I lost my mom, remember?" she said.

"I'm so sorry, Harriet," said the hare. "I do apologize. I wasn't thinking what I was saying.

Too fond of the sound of my own voice—that's my trouble. Will you forgive me?"

Harriet nodded.

"You didn't mean any harm," she muttered.

"On the contrary," said Wiz, "I would like to do you some good. Perhaps I'll be able to one of these fine days. And talking of fine days, I must remember to watch out for your father on his combine. I want to get back to Pars in one piece."

"Yes," said Harriet, "you must be careful, Wiz. It isn't only Dad. You might meet a poacher with a gun or with dogs, or a fox might get you in the night, or you might be run over on the road."

"Good heavens!" said the hare. "Maybe I should have been a tiger after all."

"I'm glad you're not," said Harriet, and she knelt down and stroked the hare's tawny back.

"I'm sorry I snapped at you, Wiz," she said.

"I deserved it," said the hare.

"We're friends again, aren't we?" Harriet said.

"Certainly," said Wiz. "You are literally my one and only friend on Earth."

He stood up on his hind legs and, turning his head slightly to one side, gazed up the hill toward the farmhouse.

"Eyes on the sides of one's head are a nuisance," he said. "We Partians have three hundred and sixty degree sight—stalk-eyed, you know—and even you humans have binocular vision. But a hare, it seems, doesn't see straight ahead too well. Which is your bedroom?"

"The right-hand one of the three upper windows," said Harriet. "That's mine."

"I might come up and pay you a visit sometime," said Wiz.

"But how? Hares can't climb up walls."

"I'm an unusual hare."

"Well, for goodness' sake, don't let Dad or our dog Bran catch sight of you."

"They won't see me," said Wiz, "but I'll be seeing you." And he lolloped away across the field.

CHAPTER THREE

For a couple of days Harriet saw nothing of Wiz. From her window she could spot the occasional rabbit in the valley below, but she saw no hare, European or Partian. She rode across the farm on Breeze, now and again calling "Wiz! Wiz!" But no one answered.

"Wish you could talk like he does," she said to the pony. "We could have such interesting conversations." Breeze blew a bubbly snort of agreement.

"At least," said Harriet, "I can tell you all about Wiz. That's not breaking my promise to him, because even though you can understand a lot of things I say, I doubt that a magic hare from outer space would mean much to you. And I can't talk about it to Dad or Mrs. Wisker, the cleaning lady, or the postman or the vet, and I haven't got

a mom to tell even if I could. I wish I did—have
a mom, I mean. It must be nice."

That evening, when her father came up to say
good night to her, Harriet said, "Dad, d'you think
you'll ever get married again?"

Her father sat down on the bed.

"Would you be pleased if I did, Hattie?" he
asked.

"Well, yes, I suppose so. If it was someone you liked."

"Only liked?"

"Well, loved, then."

Harriet's father took hold of her hand and idly tickled the palm of it with one finger, just as he used to when she was little.

"I don't think it's very likely," he said. "Just because Mommy's not here anymore doesn't mean I've stopped loving her. And anyway, I don't meet anybody much, do I?"

"No."

"I don't like to think of you being lonely."

"I'm not a bit lonely," said Harriet. "I've got you and Breeze and Bran and all the other animals."

She yawned.

"And Wiz," she said sleepily.

"Who's Wiz?" said her father.

"Oh," said Harriet. "Oh . . . that's my nickname for Mrs. Wisker."

Mrs. Wisker was a stout middle-aged widow, thorough but not the world's fastest worker.

"Funny name for her," said Harriet's father.

"You don't call her that to her face, do you?"

"Oh, no," said Harriet. "She might not like it. But I like her—she's nice, isn't she?"

"Perhaps I'd better marry her, then?"

"Oh, Dad!"

That night Harriet dreamed about Wiz. He had somehow climbed up to her bedroom window and come in.

When she woke, she got out of bed and leaned on the window sill to scan the valley below, but it was hareless.

There was a house martin's nest in the eaves just over her window, and she watched one of the parent birds returning from hawking insects. It swooped up with a beakful, just a few feet away from her face, and she could hear the chirping of the hungry youngsters in their cup-shaped nest of mud above.

As the martin wheeled away again, a sparrow fluttered out of the vine on the house wall and landed on the sill right beside Harriet and chirped at her.

"Cheeky thing!" she said, expecting it to fly off at the sound of her voice so close. But instead it flew past her into the room. Harriet turned around to see the hare sitting up on the bedroom carpet. Of the sparrow there was no sign.

"Wiz!" cried Harriet. "How on earth did you get here?"

"Not so much on earth as off earth," said the hare. "I flew."

"You were that sparrow? You changed into it?"

"And back again, I'm glad to say. I don't think I much fancy being *Passer domesticus.*"

"More Latin?"

"Yes."

"But you'll have to fly out again. You can't just jump out the window."

"True. But next time I think I'll be a less ordinary bird. In the meantime, how are you, Harriet?"

"Quite well, thank you," said Harriet. "And you?"

"I'm really rather enjoying my vacation on Earth," said Wiz. "It's a lovely bit of country, up here on the hills of Wiltshire. Very different from Pars."

"What's Pars like?" asked Harriet.

"Absolutely flat. Not a hump nor a hollow anywhere. That's why I like it here. And I like being a hare, too—it's fun. We Partians are slow movers, but now I can run like the wind."

"Have you come across any other hares?" said Harriet.

"Since you ask, Harriet," said Wiz, "I did meet a rather attractive young doe."

"Did you speak to her?"

"Of course."

"Not in English?"

"No. In Leporine."

"Oh. So you can speak animal languages as well?"

"Certainly."

In the yard below, Bran barked.

Harriet looked out the window to see her father and the dog setting out to fetch the herd for milking.

"Well, then, what's Bran saying?" she asked.

"He's saying a number of things," said the hare. "One is a message to the cows that he's on his way. One is a greeting to your father that he's glad to be with him. And one is just a general expression of well-being: 'It's a lovely morning and I'm a healthy, happy old dog who's glad to be alive!' "

"You can't tell all that from a bark," said Harriet.

"*Oont*," said the hare.

"*Oont?*" said Harriet. "What does that mean?"

"It's a Leporine word," said Wiz. "A sort of mild protest. In this case it means 'Surely, Harriet, you don't think I'd lie to you?' "

"Actually, I don't," said Harriet. "I believe everything you tell me, Wiz. And by the way, I've got something to tell you. Dad's going to combine the wheat today."

"In that case, I must remember to make myself scarce," said the hare, "but before that, I'd better make myself into something else. Let's see—how about *Carduelis carduelis?*"

"What's that?"

"Take a look in your bird book."

Harriet took *The Field Guide to the Birds of Britain and Europe* from her shelf and looked in the index.

"I found it!" she cried after a moment. "It's a goldfinch!"

"Switt-witt-witt-witt!" piped a voice in reply. And there, perched on her bedpost, was a beautiful little bird with a scarlet, black, and white head and black and yellow wings, as colorful as the sparrow had been drab. For a few seconds it

fluttered in front of Harriet's face as though say-ing good-bye, and then it flew out the window and away.

Harriet watched the goldfinch alight in a large patch of thistles in the paddock and disappear among them. A little later, if she had not turned away to get dressed, she would have seen a hare come out of the thistle clump and lope off down the path.

After breakfast, when her father had gone out to clean the milking parlor and yards and Harriet was washing the dishes, Mrs. Wisker arrived. She always made the same remark.

"Puffed, I am," she said, "pushin' that old bike up the hill. But then 'tis lovely freewheelin' down again."

"We're going to cut the wheat on the Ten Acre today, Mrs. Wisker," Harriet said.

"Are you now, my duck? You goin' to ride on the combine?"

"I expect so. To start with, anyway."

"Rabbit pie, then, eh?" said Mrs. Wisker.

"I wish he wouldn't shoot them," said Harriet. "I think I might be a vegetarian when I grow up."

"Bad for you, that is," said Mrs. Wisker, "doin' without meat. I likes my meat. A nice fat rabbit. Or a hare. Now, a hare's lovely, my late lamented hubby always said, provided you let it get a bit ripe."

Harriet shuddered.

"Some people say that hares are witches," she said.

"Course they are, duck, everybody knows that," said Mrs. Wisker, "but that don't stop me from eating one if I gets half a chance."

"But you believe in magic, don't you, Mrs. Wisker?"

"Course I do. Anyone with any sense does, stands to reason. Even my late lamented hubby did and he hadn't no more sense than an old sheep. How else are you goin' to account for that old circle in your dad's wheat? Got to be somethin' funny about that."

"You don't think it's due to natural causes?"

Mrs. Wisker gave a loud, piercing shriek, the sort of noise someone might make while being murdered, but Harriet knew it was only Mrs. Wisker's way of laughing.

"Natural causes, duck?" she cried. "Not on your Nelson Eddy! 'Tis spaceships as makes 'em, I reckons. UFO's, some do call 'em, but I calls 'em UHT's."

"UHT's?"

"Unnatural heavenly things!" said Mrs. Wisker with another earsplitting screech.

Later that morning, once the dew was off, combining began on the Ten Acre. A neighboring

farmer came with his tractor and trailer to help haul the grain away, while Harriet's father drove the combine harvester and she stood beside him on the platform.

At first she could see one or two rabbits moving about in the shelter of the wheat, but she knew that it was not until the uncut portion became quite small that they would begin to break from cover and make a run for it across the stubble.

"I don't want to see you shoot them, Dad!" Harriet shouted above the roar of the machine. "I don't like it. Let me get down and go home."

Thank goodness I remembered to warn Wiz, Harriet thought as she walked up the hill, hearing an occasional bang behind her. Though of course if Wiz had been in the wheat, he could have always changed himself into something else—a mole, perhaps, that would burrow down into the ground out of harm's way.

All the same, after the combining was finished, Harriet had to get up the nerve to ask her father if he had shot anything.

"Couple of bunnies," he said.

"Was that all?"

"And a hare."

Despite herself, Harriet felt a cold shiver of fear.

"Was it a buck or a doe?" she asked. Please say a doe, she thought.

"It was a buck. A big jack hare. Though I don't see what difference it makes. Either way it'll taste the same."

Harriet made herself go and look at the three bodies hanging heads-down in the back of the kitchen, two gray, one tawny. Next to the rabbits the dead hare looked very long. Its ears hung limply, and there was dried blood on its nose.

It can't be Wiz, she thought.

It *can't*.

Can it?

CHAPTER FOUR

"I'm not eating it," Harriet said at breakfast the next morning.

Her father looked up to see her spooning cornflakes into her mouth.

"Not eating what?" he asked.

"That hare you shot."

"Why not?"

"I like hares."

"Well, you like cornflakes but you eat enough of them."

"No, I don't mean 'like' like that, Daddy. Anyway, I'm not going to eat it."

"What about the rabbits?"

"Nor them."

"I was going to give them to Mrs. Wisker anyway," her father said.

"Well, give her the hare, too. Please, Dad," said Harriet.

"Hasn't it struck you," said her father, "that I might be looking forward to eating that hare? I'm very fond of jugged hare."

"Please give it away," said Harriet in a rather choky voice.

She's near tears, her father thought. Why? A woman would know, I suppose. It's not easy, trying to be a father and a mother to her.

"Okay, Hattie love," he said. "Your Wiz can have all three."

"What?"

"That's what you call Mrs. Wisker, you told me."

"Oh. Oh, yes. Thanks, Dad."

So the next time Mrs. Wisker came to Longhanger Farm, she freewheeled away down the hill again even more happily than usual. In the saddlebag of the ancient bicycle that somehow bore her weight was a hare, and a rabbit swung from each handlebar.

As for Harriet, walking around the farm or riding on Breeze, she looked with mounting impatience for her friend from Pars, so anxious had she now become to prove that he was not in Mrs. Wisker's stewpot. Even if he wasn't, he might, she told herself, have assumed some other shape as a change from being a hare. But all the animals she approached ran or hopped or flew away from her.

Until at last, a few days later, she went into the kitchen garden to get some carrots, and there was a hare helping itself to their feathery tops.

Harriet looked hastily around to make sure that neither her father nor Bran was near.

"Wiz?" she said.

"Oh, hello, Harriet," said the hare with his mouth full. "Hope you don't mind. These carrot tops are delicious."

"Where have you been?" said Harriet. "I've been so worried."

"Oh, here and there," said the hare. "What's been worrying you?"

"Dad shot a hare in the Ten Acre," said Harriet. "A buck. I just thought it might be you."

"*Oont*," said Wiz.

"What d'you mean?"

"Did you think I was that stupid? You warned me, remember? I spent that day up on the hillside—with a friend."

"I should have known it wasn't you," said

Harriet, and she bent and stroked the hare's yellowy-brown back.

At that instant Bran barked to say—the hare could have told her—"Here she is. I've found her," and Harriet turned to see her father following the dog into the kitchen garden.

"Look out, Wiz!" Harriet said out of the corner of her mouth, but when she glanced around, Wiz was nowhere to be seen.

"Going to pull some carrots?" her father asked.

"Yes."

"Something's been eating the tops, I see."

"Yes."

"Rabbits, I expect."

"I expect so."

"I'm going down to the village. Want to come?"

"Okay."

"In about five minutes, then," her father said, and walked off again.

Harriet saw a snail on the stalk of one of the chewed-off carrot tops. For a moment she wondered where on earth Wiz could have gone, but then she suddenly realized.

"I should have known it was you," said Harriet, and she bent and stroked the snail's yellowy-brown back.

She had just left the garden when there sounded a harsh, cackling cry, the alarm call of a startled blackbird. It was the first and last blackbird in the world to peck at a small, defenseless snail and then, suddenly and magically, be confronted with a large and angry hare.

That afternoon Harriet rode up to the top of the farm and out onto the open hills, where she let Breeze go wherever she pleased.

Then she saw ahead of her not one but two hares, and she reined in the pony to watch their curious antics.

They were standing on their hind legs and sparring with each other, striking out with their forefeet like boxers.

When at last they saw her, their reactions were opposite. One, the slightly larger of the two, took to its heels and raced away until it disappeared from sight. The other came hopping toward her and said "Hello!"

"Hello, Wiz," said Harriet. "Are you hurt?"

"Hurt?" said the hare.

"Well, you were fighting with that other hare and he was bigger than you."

"I wasn't fighting," said Wiz, "and it wasn't a he."

"Oh, I'm sorry," said Harriet. "I didn't mean to interrupt."

"That's all right," said Wiz. "That's the nice thing about being on vacation. There's no hurry about anything."

"How much longer are you staying?" asked Harriet. A lot longer, I hope, she thought. Things will never be the same without my magic hare.

"Well," said the hare, "return flights from Earth to Pars are always at the full moon. But let's not talk about the end of my visit. I just want to enjoy it. Come on, I'll race you."

The hillside was empty of people that July afternoon, but the hundreds of sheep grazing there stared wide-eyed at the sight of a girl on a strawberry roan pony galloping flat out over the closely nibbled turf yet never quite catching the hare that sped effortlessly in front of them.

At home that evening Harriet looked in the big diary that her father kept beside the telephone.

On July 24, the first day of her own vacation, she had put a tiny *w*. If her father had noticed it, he would have taken it for a scribble, but it stood for Wiz, marking the day she'd met him.

Today was Saturday, the last day of July.

She turned the page and there, to her dismay, it said:

MONDAY, AUGUST 2
BANK HOLIDAY (SCOTLAND)
HOLIDAY (REPUBLIC OF IRELAND)
◯ FULL MOON

"Oh, no!" Harriet said. "Is Wiz here for only two more days?"

She turned the pages. The next full moon was on September 1. On which date would Wiz leave?

All through Sunday she looked for the hare to ask him, but by the evening of the Monday when the moon would be full she still had not, as far as she knew, set eyes on him in any shape or form.

She woke in the middle of that night and went to the window to look out at the great pale disk sailing across the sky with, it seemed to her, the shape of a hare on it.

Tomorrow would he be on the way to Pars or still on Longhanger Farm?

Tuesday was one of Mrs. Wisker's days, and when she arrived and had mopped her large red face and had said what she always said, she added something extra.

"What d'you think, duck?" she said to Harriet. "When I was comin' up the path just now, I looked out in the paddock and I could see a shape there, down in the grass. Well, I remembered what my late lamented hubby always used to say. 'If you sees a shape in the grass,' he said, 'and when you walks toward it, it gets lower and lower, then 'tis an old hare. If it gets higher and higher as you walks toward it, then 'tis only a lump of muck.' Well, I leans the old bike against the fence and I climbs over and I walks toward this shape, and the nearer I gets, the lower it gets. And sure enough, it was an old hare. But here's the funny thing, my duck. 'Stead of runnin' off, that hare sits up as bold as brass and looks me in the eye. 'Get along with you,' I says, and then—would you believe it—he says somethin' back."

"What!" cried Harriet. "What?" she said.

"Well," said Mrs. Wisker, " 'twasn't a proper word, of course. Fancy a hare speakin' English!" And she let out one of her deafening screeches.

"But what was it the hare said?" asked Harriet.

"Sounded like *'oont,'* " said Mrs. Wisker. "Hey, where are you goin', duck?" But Harriet was already out the door.

Down the path she ran pell-mell, and there, calmly cropping the grass of the paddock, was her hare.

"Oh, Wiz!" she cried. "They didn't come for you, then! You're here for another whole month!"

"Certainly," said the hare. "Among other things, I promised to do you a good turn one of these days, remember? I still need a bit of time to organize it."

"Organize what?" asked Harriet.

"A nice surprise, Harriet."

"What? Tell me! Please!"

"No, no," said Wiz. "That might spoil things. You'll just have to wait and see."

CHAPTER FIVE

A little lane ran through the bed of the valley, a lane that led to nowhere except Longhanger Farm, and Harriet now heard a car coming along it and slowing down for the sharp turn into the farm's driveway.

At the sound of it Wiz loped off, and Harriet climbed back over the paddock fence. The car stopped by her and a woman stuck her head out the window. "Excuse me, but do you have any hens?" she asked.

"Yes," Harriet said.

"I wonder if you could sell me a dozen eggs?"

"Well, we just keep them for ourselves," said Harriet, "but I expect I can find you a dozen. The hens are laying quite well at the moment."

"That's very kind of you," said the woman, smiling. "What's your name, by the way?"

"Harriet Butler."

"Jump in, Harriet, and I'll drive you back up to the farm."

"Who was that, Mrs. Wisker?" Harriet asked after the woman had paid for the tray of eggs and had driven away again.

"New," said Mrs. Wisker. "Bought the old turnpike cottage t'other side of the village. Married woman, she is."

"How d'you know?"

"Got a big old gold weddin' ring on, hadn't she?"

"I didn't notice," Harriet said.

"I did!" said Mrs. Wisker with a shriek. "There's not much I don't notice, my late lamented hubby used to say. And I'll tell you another thing I knows about her, too."

"What?"

"She likes an egg for her breakfast," said Mrs. Wisker, screaming yet more loudly.

"Here's £1.50, Dad," Harriet said when her father came in at lunchtime.

"What for?"

"Eggs. I sold a dozen to a lady who came by. She's bought the old turnpike cottage, Mrs. Wisker said."

"Perhaps we should get a few more birds," said Harriet's father, "and then you could earn yourself a bit of pocket money selling eggs."

"But you pay for all the food."

"But you do all the work. Here, take this money back for a start."

*   *   *

45

"Look what I've got!" said Harriet to her hare when she met him as she rode on the hillside that afternoon.

"Money!" said Wiz. "The root of all evil."

"Well, everybody needs some," Harriet said.

"Hares don't."

"But you must have money on Pars."

"Oh, yes. But we treat it sensibly. Here on Earth some human beings have so much money they don't know what to do with it, and some are desperately poor. On Pars everyone's equal. Much fairer."

"Are you looking forward to going back?" Harriet asked.

"It'll be nice to see my friends again," said the hare.

"Have you got a lot?"

"We're all friends on Pars. There's no such word as 'enemy' in the language."

"I'm your friend, aren't I, Wiz?"

"Certainly," said the hare, and Breeze whinnied loudly.

"What's she saying?" asked Harriet.

"She's saying, 'Why are we standing here

while you chatter away with that old hare, when we could be having a good gallop?' Come on."

"You always win," said Harriet. "You're faster than Breeze."

"All right," said Wiz, "we'll make it a handicap. Go on, off you go."

Any moment now he'll pass me, thought Harriet as she urged the pony on, but no hare appeared beside her. When at last she drew rein, she looked around, but there was no sign of Wiz. She rode back, puzzled, and after a while she came upon a hedgehog waddling along.

"What are you doing up here in the hills?" she said, and the hedgehog gave a kind of grunt.

Harriet rode a little farther looking for Wiz, but then she heard a voice behind her.

"You won," said the voice, and turning the pony around, Harriet saw not a hedgehog but a hare.

"It *was* you!" she said, laughing. "A sparrow, a goldfinch, a snail, and now a hedgehog. What will you turn into next, I wonder?"

"A Partian on the next full moon," said the hare.

"I'll miss you," said Harriet. "I told Dad I wasn't lonely here on the farm, but I will be when you're gone and it's just the two of us again."

"*Oont*," said the hare.

"Why, what did I say wrong?"

"You'll see before long, sure as eggs is eggs."

"That's what I got that money for," said Harriet. "I sold some eggs to a lady who came to the farm. Dad says we can get some more hens, and then I can sell a lot."

"Perhaps she'll come back for more, this lady," said Wiz.

"She might."

"She will."

"How do you know?"

"Hares are witches, aren't they?"

By the time the newcomer to the village came again to Longhanger Farm, Mrs. Wisker had found out a lot more about her.

"She's a book writer," she told Harriet. "Writes little books for kiddies, they say, though she's got no children of her own. Mrs. Lambert, she's called, but there ain't no sign of Mr. Lambert yet. I expect she's gettin' the old place straight first. Anyway, she seems to like your eggs, my duck. Goin' to come regular, she said, didn't she?"

"Yes," said Harriet. "She's my first customer."

The next time that Mrs. Lambert came to the farm to buy eggs was not on one of Mrs. Wisker's days.

"All alone, Harriet?" she said when the door was opened.

"Yes. Dad's plowing the Ten Acre."

"I think I must have seen him as I came along the lane. I saw a big green tractor. May I have some more of your big brown eggs, please, Harriet? By the way, I should have said my name is Lambert, Jessica Lambert."

"You write stories for children, don't you?" asked Harriet as she was putting the eggs into a tray.

"Yes, for very young children."

"What about?"

"Animals, mostly. Possibly your mother read you one or two of my books when you were little?"

"I wouldn't know," Harriet said. "She died when I was very small."

"Oh. Sorry. I didn't know."

"That's all right," said Harriet.

Little did she think, as she watched her customer drive away, that she would see her again so soon. For not ten minutes later the doorbell rang again, and there on the step stood Mrs. Lambert, a bloodstained handkerchief held to her nose.

"What happened?" cried Harriet.

"I've had a bit of an accident," Mrs. Lambert

said. "I had to swerve suddenly in the lane, and
the car went into the ditch and I banged my face.
It's nothing much, just a nosebleed, I think, that's
all, but the car's stuck and I wondered . . . d'you
think your father would come and pull me out
with his tractor?"

"Yes," said Harriet, "of course he would. I'll
go and fetch him. D'you want to wash your face?
Would you like a clean hanky?"

"Yes, please, Harriet," said Mrs. Lambert. "Then I'll go back down to the car and wait for help."

A little later Harriet's father got down from the big green tractor and held out a hand.

"John Butler," he said. "How do you do?"

"Not very well, I'm afraid," said Mrs. Lambert.

"You haven't broken your nose?"

"No, I don't think so. And I hope there's nothing broken in the car. It's just that I can't get out of the ditch because the back wheels are spinning."

"We'll soon have you out of there," said Harriet's father, busy with a rope. And sure enough, the big tractor pulled the little car out in no time at all.

"All's well that ends well," said Harriet's father as he unhitched the tow rope.

"Not quite," said Harriet. "There is something broken—in the back of the car."

"What?" said Mrs. Lambert.

"Every single egg you just bought," said Harriet.

Mrs. Lambert smiled ruefully.

"All the fault of that silly animal," she said. "I had to swerve to avoid running over it. It suddenly came out of the hedge and calmly sat up in the middle of the lane as though all it wanted was for me to go in the ditch."

"This animal," said Harriet's father. "What was it?"

"A hare."

CHAPTER SIX

Was it Wiz? Harriet thought.

What was he doing, sitting in the middle of the lane? He could have easily been run over, and then he'd have never seen Pars again.

Was it a hare? her father thought. These people who came from the town to live in the country couldn't tell a hare from a rabbit. Probably it was an old tomcat anyway.

"You're sure it was a hare?" he said.

He thinks I'm a townie who can't tell a hare from a rabbit, Mrs. Lambert thought.

"I know *Lepus europaeus occidentalis* when I see one," she said.

"I don't follow you."

"It's Latin for brown hare, Dad," said Harriet.

"How do you know that?"

"I learned it," said Harriet truthfully.

"From a book, I expect," said Jessica Lambert. "Like me. I illustrate my own little stories, you see, so I have to be careful that I know what a particular animal looks like. I don't want to make silly mistakes and end up with egg on my face."

"Speaking of which," said Harriet's father, "you must let us give you some more eggs in place of the broken ones, and more importantly, how is your face?"

"My nose is a bit sore."

"And I'm afraid you're going to have a shiner," Harriet's father said.

"What's a shiner, Dad?" asked Harriet.

"A black eye. Look here, Mrs. Lambert. You must be a bit shaken. Why don't you turn around and come on back up to the farm, and we'll find you some more eggs and give you a cup of tea."

Anyone watching would have seen quite a procession going back up the driveway to Longhanger Farm.

The little car led the way, the big tractor followed, and close behind it trotted the sheepdog Bran. Far behind Bran a hare came loping up the hill.

Just as he reached the yard, some instinct made the dog turn his head to look back, but all he saw was an old crow hopping around, crying "Caark!" at him.

"Please sit down, Mrs. Lambert," said the farmer. "And put the kettle on, please, Hat."

"Isn't it awful," said Mrs. Lambert, "the way we all get our names shortened?"

"You can't shorten mine much," said John Butler.

"No! But what I mean is . . . For example, my name is Jessica—and please stop calling me Mrs. Lambert—which is quite a nice name, I think, as is Harriet. But my husband always called me Jess, which sounds like a sheepdog."

"It sounds nice enough to me," said Harriet's father.

"I'd rather you called me Jessica."

"If you call me John."

"It's a deal."

"What's a deal?" asked Harriet, coming back from the kitchen. "I hope you're not making Mrs. Lambert pay for some more eggs, Daddy. It's my fault the first dozen got broken."

"Your fault?" said Mrs. Lambert.

"Well, yes, in a way. It was my hare that caused the accident."

"Your hare?" said her father.

"Well . . . I mean . . . our hare. A Longhanger Farm hare."

"A crazy hare," said her father. "There must be a story there for you, Jessica! *The Mad Hare of Longhanger Farm.*"

As Mrs. Lambert drove away again with half a dozen fresh eggs for which Harriet would take no payment, she suddenly saw a hare (*the* hare? she thought) squatting by the side of the driveway.

She slowed down to an absolute crawl, watching the hare like a hawk. She leaned out the window and said, "You're not going to do anything silly, are you?"

To her surprise the animal made a soft but distinct noise in reply. It sounded like *"Oont."*

"She's nice, isn't she, Dad?" Harriet was saying.

"Very," said her father.

Why, he thought, did she say "My husband always *called* me Jess?"

"I suppose Mr. Lambert will turn up before long," he said in an offhand way. "I imagine she's getting the old cottage straight first."

"That's what Mrs. Wisker said."

"There's not much she doesn't notice."

"As her late lamented hubby used to say," said Harriet, and they both laughed.

When Mrs. Wisker arrived the next day, Harriet told her the whole story of the accident.

"Poor soul!" said Mrs. Wisker. "And got a black eye, too! Not the first she's had, from what I hear."

"What do you mean?" asked Harriet.

"That husband of hers. Free with his fists, they say, specially when he'd had a drop too much, which was often."

"How horrible!" said Harriet.

"He won't do it no more, duck. She got rid of him, for good and all."

"Murdered him, d'you mean?"

Mrs. Wisker gave one of her loudest shrieks.

"You been watchin' too much television," she said. "No—dee-vorced him. Couple of years ago."

The last thing that day Harriet was leaning out her bedroom window, scanning the valley below, as usual.

The evening sunshine lay warmly on the fields and on the sheep and cows that grazed in them or lay and chewed their cud. It turned to a purplish color the furrows of the newly plowed Ten Acre, where not long ago she had first seen the wheat circle.

A few rabbits hopped about in the headlands of the pastures, but there was no sign of a hare.

So still did Harriet keep that a sparrow alighted on the window sill, but when she said "Wiz?" it flew hastily away again.

Her father came in to say good night.

"Dad," she said, "you know Mrs. Lambert."

"Yes."

"Well, Mrs. Wisker says she's divorced."

"Oh, really?"

"Yes. Dad, can I ask you something?"

"Yes."

"When are we going to get some more hens?"

CHAPTER SEVEN

For a few days Harriet saw no sign of her hare.

She had plenty to occupy her anyway, because, rather to her surprise, her father had lost no time in buying her a dozen pullets at the point of lay.

So Harriet was busy admiring them and accustoming them to the rest of the flock and enjoying the excitement of collecting their very first, rather small, eggs. In addition, she had made a sign and painted on it in large letters:

FRESH FREE-RANGE FARM EGGS FOR SALE

HARRIET BUTLER

LONGHANGER FARM

She put up the notice at the end of the lane where it joined the road, and afterward she walked down there several times just to admire it.

Coming back one morning she looked over a gate at the herd, which was grazing in a lane-side field, and saw that there was one beast standing all by itself in a far corner, a long way from the others.

Harriet was not a farmer's daughter for nothing. She knew that if a cow isolates itself in this way, it very often means either that it is going to give birth or that it is ill. She climbed over the fence and went to look at it.

Harriet knew the entire herd by name—Bluebell the head cow and her special crony Buttercup, and Dahlia and Rose and Pansy and all the rest. Each had different markings that she knew, but she did not recognize this solitary cow.

Was it a neighbor's cow that had somehow gotten in with the Longhanger herd? Was it a new one that her father had recently bought? She could not see any numbered sale ticket stuck on its rump.

"Who are you?" she said as she reached it. "And what's the matter? You seem healthy enough, and you certainly don't look as if you're going to calve. Why aren't you grazing with the others? Off your food, are you?"

Since the cow made no reply to any of these questions, Harriet looked around for something to tempt it with. She saw a nice patch of white clover and bent to pull a bunch of it.

"Try this, old girl," she said, straightening up again.

"Less of the 'old girl,' Harriet," said Wiz, "and hold that clover a bit lower, will you. I'm not as tall as I was."

"Oh, Wiz!" cried Harriet. "Why did you turn yourself into a cow?"

"Just to see if I liked it."

"And did you?"

"Not a lot. I've tried being quite a few different animals since we last met, but there's nothing to touch a hare."

"Something jolly nearly did touch a hare the other day," said Harriet. "What were you doing sitting in the middle of the lane like that? It was you, wasn't it?"

"Certainly."

"Well, to begin with, you could have been killed."

"To end with, you mean. But I wasn't."

"And Mrs. Lambert might have been badly hurt."

"But she wasn't."

"What were you playing at, Wiz?"

"Judge not the play before the play be done," said the hare.

"I don't understand."

"You will. Trust me, Harriet. I know what is best for you."

Harriet sat down on the ground and chewed a piece of grass and watched the hare eat the clover.

"Before long, my vacation will be halfway through," she said.

"Mine too," said the hare. "The waxing moon will before long be full, and then I shall go."

"I don't want you to," Harriet said. "I shall be very unhappy never to see you again."

"On the contrary," said Wiz. "You are going to be very happy. And though perhaps you may not see me again, you will always be reminded of me throughout your life, perhaps as many as a thousand times, if you live to be a very old woman."

"How?"

"By looking at each full moon. You will always see the shape of a hare upon it."

"Because of you," Harriet said, "hares will always be my favorite animals."

"Ah, Harriet!" said Wiz. "You will always be my favorite human being."

At this point they heard a car coming along the lane toward the farm.

"I must go, Wiz," Harriet said. "It might be someone wanting eggs."

"Or someone bringing you a present?" said the hare.

It's not my birthday, thought Harriet as she ran back across the field, so why would anyone be bringing me a present? And how could Wiz possibly know anyway?

By the time she reached the bottom of the farm driveway the car was coming back down again, and she could see that it was Mrs. Lambert's.

"Did you want eggs?" Harriet asked.

"No, not yet," said Jessica Lambert, "though I saw your fancy new sign. No, I came to see you, but your Mrs. Wisker said you'd gone out somewhere. She seemed very interested in what's left of my black eye. You must have told her all about it."

"Yes. I'm glad it's better. What did you want to see me for?"

"To give you a present."

That Wiz, thought Harriet. He's magic.

"It's for both of you, really," said Jessica Lambert. "For you and your father. Just to say thank you for rescuing me the other day." And she held a small flat package out the car window.

"Good luck with the egg business, Harriet!" she said, and drove off.

"That Mrs. Lambert's been," said Mrs. Wisker when Harriet came into the farmhouse. "Lookin' for you, she was."

"I met her," Harriet said.

Mrs. Wisker looked at the package.

"Present?" she said.

"Yes."

"Not your birthday, is it, duck?"

"No."

"Somethin' for your dad, is it?"

"I expect so," Harriet said.

Mrs. Wisker let out a loud screech.

"What you means is 'Mind your own business and get on with your cleanin', Mrs. Wisker,' and that's what I'd better be doin'. Too nosy by half, I am, my late lamented hubby used to say."

Harriet longed to be nosy, too, to open the package and see what was in it. But it's for Dad as well, she said to herself, and she waited until Mrs. Wisker had freewheeled off and her father had come in for his lunch.

"Mrs. Lambert came again this morning," she said.

"More eggs?"

"No. This."

"What is it?"

"A present for us," she said. "Open it, Dad."

"You open it, Hat."

Carefully Harriet undid the wrapping paper.

"It feels like a framed picture," she said. Then she said, "Oh, look, Dad!"

It was a beautifully detailed little portrait of a hare.

The artist had caught precisely the slightly shorter head and redder shoulders of the jack hare, and there was a look of high intelligence in the prominent brown eye.

In the bottom right-hand corner were two tiny initials—J.L.—and opposite in very small print was the creature's Latin name.

"How lovely," said Harriet's father. "But why would she go to so much trouble?"

"Because we helped her when she had her accident," said Harriet.

"Look, she's even put *Lepus europaeus accidentalis!*"

"It's wonderfully lifelike," said her father. "Somehow it's not just any old hare but rather a very special one."

"Yes," said Harriet. "It is."

CHAPTER EIGHT

Harriet was cantering Breeze across a stretch of hills when she saw a hare behaving in an odd way.

It was leaping around and around in a circle, kicking up its heels.

As Harriet drew near, the hare stopped this strange behavior and sat awaiting her, so she knew it must be Wiz.

"What were you doing?" she said.

"Just skipping around," said Wiz.

"Why?"

"*Joie de vivre.*"

"Is that French?"

"*Oui.*"

"What does it mean?"

"The joy of living. I'm just glad to be alive. You're dead for a long time, you know."

I'm glad I won't see you dead, standing up-

right in a bottle, thought Harriet. You wouldn't
look like a hare, of course. You'd look like a Partian, and I'm quite glad I don't know what Partians look like.

"But you're not going to die for ages, are you,
Wiz?" she said.

"Hope not," said the hare. "I want to cram in
a lot more vacationing before I'm bottled."

"On Earth?"

"Perhaps."

"On Longhanger Farm?"

"Who knows? If I don't return for some time,

you won't be here anymore. You'll be living somewhere else, married probably, with a pack of kids."

"Have you got any children, Wiz?"

"On Pars, you mean?"

"Yes."

"No."

"Well, you couldn't possibly have any children on Earth, could you now?" said Harriet, but the hare did not reply.

Harriet sighed.

"It's a funny thing about vacations," she said, "but once you get about halfway through them, the rest of the time simply flies. Before you know it, I'll be back at school and you'll have left. The next full moon is on September first. That's less than a couple of weeks away now."

"Time for lots of surprises," said Wiz.

As usual, he was right.

To begin with, on the very next day Harriet had three new egg customers.

"We can't have anything eggy to eat today, Dad," she said to her father. "I sold them all."

"The pullets' eggs as well?"

"Yes. I charged much less for them, of course, because they're still rather small."

"Quite the businesswoman."

"Yes, but I'm worried about my first customer. Suppose she wants some?"

"Jessica Lambert, d'you mean?"

Harriet nodded.

"Well, she'll just have to buy some from the village shop. I'll tell her. I'm going down there this evening."

"What for?"

"To thank her for the picture of the hare, of course. You coming?"

"Callin' on Mrs. Lambert, were you, duck?" said Mrs. Wisker the next morning.

"How did you know?" said Harriet.

Mrs. Wisker gave one of her screams.

"She don't drive a Land Rover," she said, "and there was one parked outside the old turnpike cottage yesterday evenin'. Anyway, I seen you comin' out. Hour and twenty-three minutes you was there. Nice, was it?"

"Yes," said Harriet. "She showed me all the

books she's written. She does the pictures, too, you know."

"Like that one of a hare you got in the livin' room?"

"You don't miss much, Mrs. Wisker, do you?" said Harriet.

"Only my late lamented hubby!" said Mrs. Wisker with another screech.

One thing you don't know, thought Harriet, is that Dad's asked Mrs. Lambert to dinner this coming Saturday. And he's going to cook seven-hour lamb, and I'm going to make a fresh fruit salad, and I'm going to be allowed to stay up really late.

The weather was perfect that Saturday evening, August twenty-first. They sat out in the warmth of the old walled garden at the back of the farm-house, and Mrs. Lambert and Harriet's father drank wine, and Harriet drank Coke, and Bran ate dog biscuits in the sunshine.

Almost the first thing that happened was that Mrs. Lambert said to Harriet, in the nicest way, with the nicest smile, "Harriet, you must stop calling me Mrs. Lambert, d'you understand?"

"Yes, Jessica," said Harriet, and they all laughed comfortably.

And the seven-hour lamb, with lots of vegetables from the garden, was beautifully tender, and the fresh fruit salad was perfectly delicious, and everybody happily ate too much.

"Time you went to bed, Hat," said John Butler at last.

"But Dad," said Harriet, "you promised I could stay up really late."

"You already have," said her father. "It's past eleven o'clock."

In bed Harriet lay and thought how strange it was to hear the murmur of voices in the room below, and how nice it was that her dad had someone grown up to talk to.

A little later she heard the voices outside below her open window.

"Thank you so much, John. It's been a perfect evening," said one voice.

"Thank you for coming, Jessica," said the other voice.

Then, after a brief pause, Harriet heard a car

door shut and an engine start. The noise of it fell away as the car went down the hill, and Harriet fell asleep.

When she woke up the next morning, there was the hare sitting beside the bed.

"How did you get in here?" she asked.

"Sparrow again," said Wiz. "I couldn't be bothered with anything fancy. Just dropped by to see how your dinner party went."

"How did you know?" Harriet said. "You're worse than Mrs. Wisker."

"I know lots of things that you don't know I know," said Wiz. "Like what's going to happen on Thursday, for example."

"What is going to happen?"

"A surprise. I told you there'd be surprises."

Harriet looked at the calendar hanging on the wall by her bed.

"Thursday's the twenty-sixth," she said, but she found herself talking to a sparrow that chirped at her and flew out the window.

Later that morning the phone rang.

"Longhanger Farm," said Harriet.

"Oh, Harriet, it's Jessica. Is your father there?"

"No, he's out in the yard somewhere."

"Doesn't matter, you can ask him later. The thing is, I've got to go up to London to see my publisher this week, and I wondered if you would like to come with me? We could go and see some of the sights and generally have a day out, if you'd like to."

"I'd love to, Jessica!" said Harriet. "I'll ask Dad if I can. What day?"

"Thursday. That's the twenty-sixth."

"D'you want to go?" Harriet's father said when she asked him.

"Oh, yes, please!"

"You like Jessica, don't you?"

"Of course. Don't you?"

John Butler smiled.

"You give her a call," he said, "and tell her it's okay by me. I'm sure you'll have a lovely day."

And they did.

They drove to the station and got on the train, something Harriet had rarely ever done before. Then, when they reached London, Harriet was taken in to the publisher's offices, where they made a fuss over her. And then Harriet and Jessica saw the Changing of the Guard at Bucking-ham Palace and had a lovely lunch and went to the Natural History Museum and Madame Tussaud's and last of all, to the planetarium, where Harriet looked in vain for the planet Pars.

It's too far away, she said to herself. They haven't discovered it yet. I'm the only person who knows about it.

By the time they arrived back at Longhanger Farm the afternoon milking was finished and the herd was coming down the path, Bluebell at the head, Bran and his master behind.

They waited until the cows had gone past and then they got out of the car and crossed the lane to join the farmer and lean on the gate—the man on the top bar, the woman on the second, the child on the third—and watch the big black-and-white animals fanning out across the sunlit meadow.

"Good day, Hat?" asked Harriet's father.

"It was wonderful, Daddy," said Harriet, and she told him about all the things they'd done.

"How about you, Jessica?" asked John Butler. "How were things at your publisher?"

"Well, they seem to like my latest story."

"What's it about, Jessica?" asked Harriet's father.

"A hare. Doing that little picture for you gave me some ideas."

"Speak of the devil!" said the farmer, and he pointed at the field.

There, they saw, was a hare, leaping around and around in a circle, kicking up its heels.

"I wonder why it's behaving like that?" said Jessica.

"I don't know," said John Butler.

"I do," said Harriet. "It's *joie de vivre*."

CHAPTER NINE

It was the final weekend of Harriet's summer vacation.

"And of Wiz's, too," she said to Breeze as she was mucking out the horse stall, watched by Bran.

The pony blew through her nostrils and the dog whined softly, as though they knew how Harriet was feeling.

"Life's never going to be quite the same again without my hare," she said. "No more magic, no more surprises. He promised to do me a good turn one of these days. I suppose that must have been the trip to London with Jessica. And speaking of trips—just think how far he'll be going on Wednesday night when the moon is full. When I was in the planetarium, I looked to see which planet was the farthest away and it was Pluto, but Pars is probably ten times farther. I suppose he'll change into a Partian before he gets into the spaceship. I wonder where it will land."

Later she walked down the path and across the first field to the one beyond, where a mere five weeks ago she had seen that circle in the wheat.

Now it had been plowed and worked down and sown with a grass-seed mixture, and there was already a faint tinge of green against the brown earth.

There was something else brown, too, she could see, just where the circle had been, and because it sank as she walked toward it, she knew it was a hare and not just a lump of muck.

Not until Harriet was almost upon it did the hare spring up and run away, and she bent down and put her hand in the slight hollow left by its body and felt the warmth of it.

"Well, you weren't Wiz," she said. And a voice behind her said, "Too true."

"Oh," said Harriet to her hare, "was that a friend of yours?"

"You could say that," replied Wiz.

"I'm afraid I frightened him."

"*Oont,*" said the hare, the only word of the

Leporine language that Harriet had ever heard. It meant disapproval, she knew.

"What did I say wrong?" she asked.

"You didn't frighten him, you frightened her," said Wiz. "I tried to tell her that you wouldn't hurt her, but she has no confidence in humans. Let's hope her children grow up to be more trusting."

"Children? She has babies?"

"Her three leverets are in this field. Unlike their mother, they will not move when you approach, for she has told them to keep perfectly still. Each one has been left in a different part of the field, and when you have gone, she will go to each in turn to feed it."

"Why aren't they all in a nest together the way baby rabbits would be?" asked Harriet.

"Baby rabbits," said Wiz, "can afford to be born blind and naked and helpless, because they're safe underground. But hares live aboveground, so the leverets stand a better chance of survival if they're separated. Come, I will show you."

So Harriet followed as Wiz led her in turn to each of the three recently born babies. Like all leverets, they had come into the world with a covering of hair, open-eyed, and able to run, but they all lay as still as stone when Harriet bent and gently stroked them.

"Three little does," said Wiz.

"They're lovely!" said Harriet.

"Aren't you going to congratulate me?"

"You mean . . . ? Oh, Wiz! How wonderful! To think that when you're gone, your daughters will still be here! Will they be magic?"

"They won't talk to you or change into other creatures, if that's what you mean. But I'd like to think that maybe they'll be a little different from the average hare."

"How will I know them from other hares once they're grown?"

"Because unlike other hares, they will never run away from you. I am going to teach them that right away, now that they've seen you. They will run from any other human being or from any enemy, such as a dog or a fox. But if in time you chance upon a hare that remains lying in place and allows you to stroke it, that will be one of my daughters."

"That will be wonderful!" said Harriet.

They'll always remind me of you, Wiz, she thought as she walked home. Not that I could ever forget you.

Jessica Lambert came for eggs that afternoon, and Harriet said to her suddenly, "Do you believe in magic?"

"Of course I do," said Jessica. "Anyone with any sense does."

You sound just like Mrs. Wisker, Harriet thought.

"Can animals be magical?" she said.

"Some can," said Jessica. "Hares have always been thought to be beasts of magic."

That is exactly what Wiz said, thought Harriet.

"Dad shot one when he was combining," she said.

Jessica sighed.

"Oh, dear," she said. "I really wish he wouldn't shoot them."

And now, thought Harriet, you sound like me. "Couldn't you ask him not to?" she said.

"Why don't you?"

"He'd take more notice of you."

"Why don't we both ask him?"

So they did.

"What's all this?" John Butler said. "An anti-hunting campaign?"

"No," said Jessica. "We're not trying to keep you from getting rid of the rabbits and pigeons that damage your crops. We're just asking you not to shoot hares again."

"Ever," said Harriet.

"Why not?"

"Because," said Jessica, "we both happen to be rather fond of hares."

"I'm fond of hares, too!"

"To eat, he means!" cried Harriet, close to tears. "Please, Dad, say you won't!"

"All right, all right," said her father. "I hereby solemnly promise that I will never shoot a hare on Longhanger Farm again. Will that do?"

"Yes," they said. "That will do."

"And come on Sunday and have lunch with me, both of you," said Jessica. "I'll make you roast beef with all the trimmings."

"It seems funny," said Harriet to her father when her first customer had driven away, "to still be making Jessica pay for her eggs. I mean, you ought to give your friends things, not make them pay."

"Maybe she won't be buying them for much longer," Harriet's father said.

"Why not?"

"Oh . . . I don't know . . . she might be moving."

"Oh, I hope not!" said Harriet.

And I hope so, said her father, but he said it to himself.

CHAPTER TEN

"Penny for your thoughts, Harriet," said Jessica at the end of lunch on Sunday.

Harriet had been quiet throughout the meal, leaving the grownups to do the talking.

"She's miles away somewhere," her father said.

Soon, thought Harriet, my hare will be millions of miles away. He's got only three more days of his vacation left.

"Jessica," she said, "does your hare story have a happy ending?"

"Oh, yes," said Jessica. "I like happy endings."

"Me too," said Harriet's father, "so let me give you a hand with the dishes, and that'll be a happy ending to a lovely lunch."

"Can I help?" said Harriet.

"Actually," said her father quickly, "I was just going to ask you to do something for me, Hattie. Could you go on ahead and check on old Buttercup? She's due to calve any time now and I forgot to take a look at her as we drove down here. I won't be long. I'll probably catch up before you reach home."

"Okay," said Harriet.

Funny, she thought as she walked through the village and turned into the lane, Dad could have just as easily looked at Buttercup himself on the way back.

She went into the cow pasture and walked around the herd. Several cows were lying down, comfortably cudding, Buttercup among them.

"She doesn't look as though she had any immediate plans for calving," said a familiar voice, and there was Wiz, hopping toward her.

He knows everything about everything, thought Harriet as she squatted down to stroke her hare.

"I named you well," she said. "You're a wizard."

"And you're a very special girl, Harriet," said

the hare, "and it's nice to think that I'm going to do you that good turn I promised."

"You mean you haven't done it yet? I thought it was the London trip. Or perhaps teaching your daughters to trust me."

"No. The really big surprise that I have arranged for you is actually beginning to happen at this very minute as we speak."

"I don't understand," said Harriet.

"You will," said Wiz, "when the moon is full."

"Do you mean the surprise is that you're not leaving, after all? You're going to stay longer?"

"No, I'm going, all right. By the time you understand what I'm talking about, I'll be gone."

"But then I won't be able to thank you for whatever it is."

"I don't need thanks, Harriet. It is I who am grateful to you for making my trip to Earth such fun. All I ask you to do is to be kind to my daughters, to all hares, to all animals, for the rest of your long life."

"I will, I will!" said Harriet.

She looked earnestly into the hare's large brown eyes.

"Are you telling me that I'm going to live to be very old?" she asked.

"Certainly," replied Wiz. "You will see a thousand full moons in your time."

Harriet smiled happily.

"Oh, Wiz!" she said. "I believe every word you say."

She got to her feet and watched the hare lolloping slowly away across the pasture. Then she shouted after him, "I suppose you know exactly when old Buttercup is going to calve?"

"Certainly," said the hare. "Tuesday morning. Ten o'clock. Heifer calf." And off he went.

Harriet was just turning in to the driveway when she heard the Land Rover coming along the lane. Her father stopped. What's he looking so pleased about? she thought.

"Buttercup all right?" he asked as she got in.

"Oh, yes, she's not doing anything. I expect she'll calve about the middle of Tuesday morning."

"Oh, really?" said her father. "Perhaps you'd tell me the exact time, Miss Smarty-pants?"

"Ten o'clock. And she'll have a heifer calf."

John Butler laughed.

"Well, I hope she does," he said. "She's a good milker, old Buttercup, but she's always had bull calves. I'd like a daughter of hers."

Harriet thought of Wiz's children as the Land Rover rattled up the driveway. He seemed pleased to have daughters.

"When I was born," Harriet said, "were you glad I was a girl, Dad?"

"Very glad," said her father. "And so was your mother. Remember that old saying: 'A son is a son till he gets him a wife. A daughter's a daughter the rest of her life.' "

My long life, thought Harriet. I suppose if I asked, Wiz could tell me all sorts of things that are going to happen to me, but I don't want to know. All I want for now is just to be here on Longhanger Farm with my dad.

She looked at his strong hand on the steering wheel and put hers on top of it.

"Are you happy, Dad?" she asked.

"Very happy, Hat," he said. "Why do you ask? Don't tell me you can predict my future as well as Buttercup's?"

He laughed again.

"A heifer calf at exactly ten o'clock on Tuesday morning!" he said. "Pigs might fly!"

The next day, Monday, August thirtieth, Harriet was clearing away the breakfast things when Mrs. Wisker arrived.

"Puffed, I am," she said, "pushin' that old bike up the hill. But then 'tis lovely freewheelin' down again. I just hope it don't come on to rain. We shall get some sure enough—the cows is all lyin' down and there was a red sky this mornin' and the swallows is all flyin' low. Oh, and I tell you what, duck—I seen that old hare again just now as I was comin' up. Sittin' up bold as brass, it was."

"Did he say anything to you?" asked Harriet.

Mrs. Wisker gave her usual earsplitting shriek of laughter.

"Say anything?" she cried. "Oh, you're a scream, you are, duck!"

It's you that's the scream, thought Harriet.

"Is the hare still there?" she asked.

"Far as I know," said Mrs. Wisker. "You want to tell your dad to get his gun? He gave me a lovely hare, harvesttime."

When Harriet walked down the path, she

found Wiz feeding quietly beside the fence.

"Did you want me?" she said.

"Yes," said the hare. "Just to give you a weather warning. Were you thinking of going riding today?"

"Yes, I was. I thought I'd ride up to the hillside this morning and we could have a race. But don't be a hedgehog this time."

"Don't go," said the hare, "unless you want to risk being struck by lightning. There's going to be a humdinger of a thunderstorm in a couple of hours. Come tomorrow morning instead. I'll look out for you."

"All right," said Harriet. "But not till the afternoon. I want to see Dad's face when Buttercup's calf arrives."

Even as the hare loped off, Harriet heard a rumble of thunder in the far distance, and by the time Mrs. Wisker had finished her cleaning and was ready to go home, the storm was banging and crashing right overhead, with lightning to match.

"I'm not goin' in that," said Mrs. Wisker. "The old bike might get struck, and then it wouldn't only be my hubby as was late lamented, 'twould be me, too.'' And she waited an extra hour, flicking a duster about, until the storm had passed.

On the following morning, the last day of August, Harriet's father came in for breakfast after the morning milking and said, ''I'm beginning to wonder if you're going to be right.''

''What about, Dad?'' asked Harriet.

''Old Buttercup's thinking about calving. I left her out in the pasture when I brought the rest of the herd in.''

''I'll meet you down there at ten o'clock sharp,'' said Harriet.

And at ten o'clock sharp, as father and daughter stood and watched, Buttercup dropped a fine heifer calf.

''Dad was really amazed!'' shouted Harriet that afternoon as Breeze galloped across the hillside, the hare running alongside.

''Your turn next!'' cried Wiz, and he sprinted ahead to win the race easily.

''My turn next? What did you mean?'' asked Harriet when she had slipped off the puffing pony.

"To be amazed," said Wiz, and no matter how much she questioned him, he would say no more.

"I cannot understand," said Harriet's father when he came to say good night at the end of the day, "how you were so sure about that calving. How did you know?"

"You wouldn't believe me if I told you, Dad," said Harriet, and no matter how much he questioned her, she would say no more, except that at last she said "Rabbits!"

It was their custom—something taught to John Butler as a boy and to his father before him—that on the last day of each month, the last word you spoke before going to sleep was "Rabbits!" and that when you woke up the next morning on the first of the new month, the first word you uttered was "Hares!" To do this was to ensure good luck.

So Harriet's father duly replied "Rabbits!" Then he kissed her and went downstairs.

"Hares!" Harriet said loudly the moment she woke on Wednesday, September first, and then her spirits sank like a stone as she remembered. Tonight the moon will be full.

Tonight she would lose her hare.

CHAPTER ELEVEN

Harriet dressed and went to let out her hens and to feed the calves. As usual, she looked in through the door of the milking parlor and called, "Morning, Daddy."

"Hares!" said her father. "You're supposed to say 'Hares.'"

"I already have."

"Oh, it's all right, then."

No, it's not all right, Harriet thought. Saying that is supposed to bring good luck, but how could it when Wiz is going?

Would she even set eyes on him again before he left?

All morning she wandered about the farm hoping to see her hare, but there was no sign of him. And when she rode throughout the hillside calling his name in the afternoon, there was no answer except the bleating of sheep, the sad cries of lapwings, and the sigh of the wind.

But when in the evening Harriet went into the kitchen garden to pick the last of the scarlet runners, she found that someone else had gotten there first.

"Hope you don't mind," said the hare, standing on his hind legs to pull down a bean pod, "but I couldn't resist a last snack."

"Don't you have vegetables on Pars?" Harriet asked.

"Heavens no! We live on synthetic additive-free low-cholesterol pills," said Wiz. "I am going to miss being a hare."

"I am going to miss you," said Harriet, "dreadfully."

Wiz bit through the bean pod with his two large front teeth and began to chew, moving his lower jaw from side to side.

"Very suitable for hares, these beans," he said.

"Why?"

"They're both runners."

Harriet watched without saying anything.

"That was supposed to be a joke," said Wiz.

"I'm sorry," said Harriet. "I don't feel like laughing."

"*Oont*," said the hare.

He swallowed his mouthful and looked directly up at her.

"Listen to me, Harriet," he said. "You mustn't feel sad. Look at it from my point of view. I'm an alien on a strange planet, and although I've had a lovely time, I'm looking forward to going home to Pars and to my friends. Of course I will miss you, but I'm happy to be going and you must be happy for me. By this time tomorrow you will be a very happy girl, indeed, let me tell you. You told me that you believed every word I said. Believe me now."

"All right," said Harriet.

She bent and stroked his tawny back.

"Stroke my children when you come upon them," said the hare, "and think of me."

"I will, Wiz," said Harriet. "But I don't want to say good-bye."

"Then don't," said the hare, and with one easy bound he leaped over the garden wall and was gone.

At the end of that first day of September, Harriet
stood at her bedroom window looking down into
the valley below and hoping for perhaps one last
glimpse of her hare, but there was no sign of him.

Already the full moon was sailing in the dark-
ening sky, and Harriet stared up at it, thinking as
she now would always think that the business of
the man in the moon was ridiculous. The image
on the great round disk was without a doubt the
outline of a hare.

Her father came in to say good night.

"You haven't sold out of eggs, have you, Hat?" he asked.

"No. Why?"

"Might need an extra one for breakfast tomorrow."

Greedy old Dad, Harriet thought. He usually never has two.

The night was a still one, and Harriet lay awake for a very long time, straining her ears for any unusual sound. When she at last fell asleep, she slept lightly, so that a distant noise woke her.

It was a rushing, tearing, swishing noise, just like the sound of fireworks, but this time it did not come from the valley below but from the opposite direction, far away, right up at the top of Longhanger Farm, up on the hillside.

Harriet sat up and looked at her watch.

It was midnight, the witching hour.

"Be happy for me" Wiz said, she thought, so I must be, and she lay down again and shut her eyes.

When she opened them again, it was to find that she had slept late.

She went to the window and saw that her father had finished the morning milking, that the herd was already in the pasture, and that a car was coming up the driveway.

Jessica's car, thought Harriet. She must be out of eggs. Harriet dressed quickly and ran downstairs.

Her father was already in the kitchen.

"Set an extra place, will you, Hattie, please?" he called. "Jessica's coming for breakfast." And with that there was a knock on the front door.

"How d'you like your boiled egg, Jessica?" Harriet's father shouted from the kitchen.

"Sort of medium, please, John. Softish yolk, firmish white, if you know what I mean."

"I do."

"That's how we like ours," said Harriet.

What's she doing here for breakfast? Harriet thought. I mean, I'm glad she's here. I like her. Come to think of it, I like her very much indeed. But why breakfast?

Not until they had finished eating did Jessica say, "You're wondering why I'm here so early in the day, aren't you, Harriet? It's because I've got some news to tell you and I couldn't wait any longer."

"Oh, no!" cried Harriet. "You're moving! Dad said you might be moving."

"Yes, I am. Not for a while yet, but then I will sell the old turnpike cottage."

"Then where are you going to live?" asked Harriet.

"At Longhanger Farm," said her father.

Harriet looked blank. Her mind was still full of thoughts of Wiz, speeding away on his long, long journey to Pars, and she could not grasp what was being said.

"Last Sunday," said Jessica, "after lunch, when your father asked you to go look at Buttercup, it was because he wanted to ask me something."

"Over the dishes," said John Butler. "So romantic."

"He asked me to marry him, Harriet," said Jessica Lambert, "and I said, 'Yes, but only if Harriet approves.'"

Suddenly everything was blindingly clear to Harriet.

It was all Wiz's doing!

This was the good turn he'd promised. This was the really big surprise. He had arranged the whole thing, from the moment when he'd sat in the lane and caused Jessica to go in the ditch, so that Harriet's father could rescue her.

"Tomorrow you will be a very happy girl," he had said yesterday.

In fact, Harriet was so delighted that at first she could not speak. She jumped up from the table and dashed around it to Jessica and gave her an enormous hug. Then she gave her father another one.

At last she said, "It's like a fairy tale."

Jessica laughed.

"There's often a wicked stepmother in a fairy tale," she said, "but I'll try very hard to be a good one. And I'll start by letting you off from washing the dishes, Harriet. Or may I call you Hattie, too, now?"

"Whatever you like," Harriet said happily.

And she sat by herself for a while at the breakfast table after her father and Jessica had cleared it. She listened to the sounds of talk and laughter

coming from the kitchen and thought how nice it was going to be for both of them. For Jessica, after that awful first husband who called her Jess like a sheepdog and knocked her around, and for her father, after almost six long lonely years.

She stared up at the portrait hanging on the wall.

To Jessica, to her father, to Mrs. Wisker, or to anyone else, it was just a very good likeness of a hare.

But to her and her alone, it was a portrait of a wizard, of a beast of magic who for a thousand full moons to come would remain, as he had always been, Harriet's hare.

ABOUT THE AUTHOR

Dick King-Smith was born and raised in Gloucestershire, England. He served in the Grenadier Guards during World War II, then returned home to Gloucestershire to realize his lifelong ambition of farming. After twenty years as a farmer, he turned to teaching and then to writing the children's books that have earned him many fans on both sides of the Atlantic. Inspiration for his writing comes from his farm and his animals.

Among his well-loved novels are *Babe: The Gallant Pig*, *Harry's Mad*, *Martin's Mice* (each an American Library Association Notable Book); *Ace: The Very Important Pig* (a *School Library Journal* Best Book of the Year); *The Toby Man*, *Paddy's Pot of Gold*, *Pretty Polly*, *The Invisible Dog*, and *Three Terrible Trins*. Additional honors and awards he has received are a *Boston Globe–Horn Book* Award (for *Babe: The Gallant Pig*) and the California Young Reader Medal (for *Harry's Mad*). In 1992 he was named Children's Author of the Year at the British Book Awards.